DOGS ★ ON ★ DUTY

DOROTHY HINSHAW PATENT

SOLDIERS' BEST FRIENDS ON THE **BATTLEFIELD** AND **BEYOND**

WALKER & COMPANY ✹ NEW YORK

★ When Are Dogs Also SEALs?

When people learned that a dog had been a key team member of Navy SEAL Team Six in the successful raid on Osama bin Laden's compound in May 2011, everyone wanted to know more about the dog. What was its role in the attack? What breed of dog was it, and what was its name? While the navy remained quiet about details of the raid for security reasons, we do know that the dog's name is Cairo. He is a Belgian Malinois (MAL-in-wah), a breed especially well suited to military use.

A US Army soldier and his dog jump
from an aircraft over the Gulf of Mexico during training.

A Special Forces dog may wear a vest like this to protect it and to provide its handler with information about what it encounters on its mission.

The Special Forces, such as Navy SEALs, are only one branch of the military that use dogs as important parts of their teams. Military Working Dogs (MWDs) are now vital members of all the armed forces. War dogs have come a long way since humans first used them thousands of years ago. Back then they were weapons of fear, released by the hundreds in front of armies to terrify and disable the enemy.

Today, they help keep servicemen and women safe from the hidden explosives planted by invisible enemies who aim to kill and disable our troops. They guard military bases and search naval ships for explosives. Sometimes they wear special equipment that can both protect them from harm and provide vital information to their handlers. They can learn to jump fearlessly from high-flying planes and parachute to the ground in remote locations, and to scramble over piles of unstable rubble to find hidden explosives.

Ronnie, a Belgian Malinois, is prepared to be hoisted up into a helicopter in Afghanistan.

What Makes Dogs So Special?

Dogs are unlike any other animal. They have become partners with the military largely because of their special senses. Dogs' night vision enables them to warn of sneak attacks, which are a serious threat to soldiers. Dogs' ears can also detect sounds well above the human range of hearing, and their sense of smell is far superior to that of humans. These "super" senses, combined with their natural protective instincts, have earned them the job of guarding military camps for as long as humans have fought one another. Dogs also form a strong emotional connection with people, giving them a natural desire to work with and please their human friends. Because of all these special abilities, dogs can be trained to play many roles in our lives, including helping keep our forces safe during wartime.

The K9 Storm Vest camera has night-vision ability for searching in dark places.

US Army MWD Andy searches through rubble and trash to locate weapons or explosives.

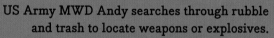
This Doberman keeps guard while his handler manages a quick nap during the World War II battle of Iwo Jima.

7

A wounded British soldier removes a bandage from a Red Cross dog's pack.

The war dogs used in ancient times to intimidate the enemy originated with this giant breed, the Tibetan Mastiff.

It has taken time, however, for people to appreciate just how useful dogs can be for the armed forces. From the ancient days of vast conquering armies in Europe to today's small patrol units of American forces and their allies searching for enemy fighters and weapons, war dogs have evolved through many stages. In World War I they served as Red Cross dogs, seeking out the wounded and bringing them aid, and as messengers, bravely dodging through the trenches to deliver critical information between command posts and the front.

Messenger dogs gave soldiers on the battlefield a way to share information with their officers during World War I.

WORLD WAR I HERO HOUND: STUBBY

Stubby was the most famous American war dog of World War I. An American soldier named Robert Conroy found Stubby wandering the streets of Hartford, Connecticut. Conroy smuggled Stubby aboard the ship that took his division to France. At that time, dogs weren't considered a part of the military, but Stubby won over the authorities by learning the drills and performing a doggie salute, lifting his right paw above his eye whenever the soldiers saluted.

Stubby was a natural guard dog who saved Conroy and the other men more than once. His superb sense of smell alerted him to a nighttime poisonous gas attack, giving the troops precious seconds to don their gas masks. Another time he caught a German soldier by the pants as he was trying to get into camp. Stubby took part in many battles and would lie down beside injured men to comfort them, while barking to help medics find the wounded. He also carried messages from the front. After spending weeks in a hospital recovering from wounds he received from German grenades, he returned to the battlefield and continued to serve fearlessly. Stubby became a famous symbol of loyalty and courage.

After the war, Stubby was a celebrity, leading parades and meeting US presidents Wilson, Harding, and Coolidge. He became the football mascot at Georgetown University, where he continued to live with Conroy until his death in 1926.

Families willingly offered their beloved pets to the war effort during WWII.

★ Dogs Join the Fight

The role of dogs expanded during World War II, spearheaded initially by a civilian group called Dogs for Defense that encouraged the military to enlist family pets in the armed forces. Thousands of Americans offered their dogs for the war effort.

At first, more than thirty breeds were trained by the army, navy, and coast guard. Later on, the breed list narrowed down to seven—Belgian Sheepdogs, Doberman Pinschers, American Eskimo dogs, farm collies, German Shepherds, Malamutes, and Siberian Huskies.

These breeds were put to work in a variety of jobs. Some were messengers, while others served as base sentries or scouts who could sense the enemy's presence before the soldiers or marines could.

More than nine thousand dogs served in WWII, saving the lives of thousands of soldiers. After the war, those that survived were retrained to get used to civilian life again, and then were returned to their families or adopted by new owners.

WORLD WAR II HERO HOUND: CHIPS

A shepherd mix named Chips from a family in New York State demonstrated dramatically how dogs could save human lives in battle. As Chips and his outfit landed on a beach in Sicily, gunfire suddenly erupted. Chips wrestled himself free from his handler, charged the gun nest, and attacked the Italian soldiers. In minutes, four bitten and bleeding soldiers surrendered. Another time while under attack, Chips's handler attached a phone cable to his collar. He streaked back to base, dodging gunfire. The cable allowed the American soldiers to establish contact and request badly needed reinforcements.

These huskies are being trained to feel comfortable getting hoisted above the ground in case they'll be needed in hard-to-reach places.

Sentry dogs served in the coast guard, patrolling the shoreline for enemy submarine activity.

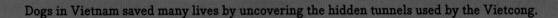

Dogs in Vietnam saved many lives by uncovering the hidden tunnels used by the Vietcong.

While dogs did play a minor role during the Korean War, it wasn't until the Vietnam War that military strategists began to realize all the ways a dog's powerful senses could be used to protect troops from harm. Dogs were critical to saving soldiers' lives during the Vietnam War when the US fought the Vietcong. Patrol dogs guarded US bases at night, when their keen vision and hearing could detect the enemy. Scout dogs went out with army and marine combat patrols along narrow trails through the dense jungle. The Vietcong dug an elaborate tunnel system, which allowed them to travel undetected beneath US troops and then come out to ambush American soldiers. The dogs could find these tunnels and even alert their handlers to the thin wires connected to booby traps. The scout dogs weren't trained to attack but provided a silent alert.

A scout dog jumps down from a helicopter in Vietnam, ready to get to work.

Two South Vietnamese soldiers cross
a river with a military working dog
during the Vietnam war.

Records show only about two hundred of the
dogs left Vietnam as the war wound down.
Officially considered to be "equipment," most
were given to the South Vietnamese Army,
which wasn't set up to accept so many dogs.
Some dogs were euthanized. But their handlers
were brokenhearted and never forgot these
brave four-legged soldiers who kept them alive
and safe.

★ ★ ★ ★

About four thousand dogs served during
that war, saving thousands of American fighters
from death or maiming. Hundreds of the dogs
died in combat. The dogs and handlers bonded
strongly, doing whatever they could to protect
each other.

Across the US, Vietnam veterans have erected monuments like this one
in Fort Benton, Montana, to honor the dogs that helped keep them safe.

14

VIETNAM HERO HOUND: NEMO

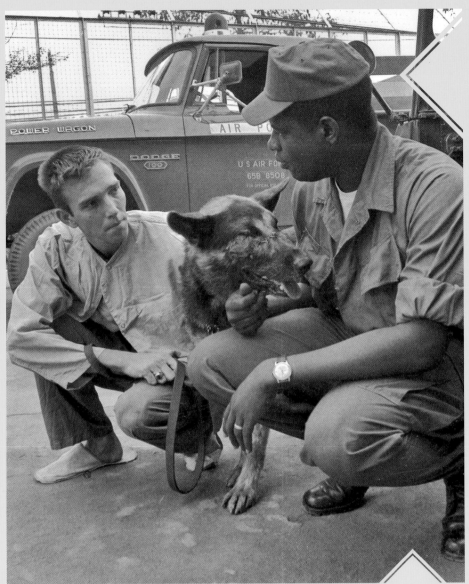

A1C Robert Thorneburg and A3C Leonard Bryant visit with Nemo shortly after the attack on Tan Son Nhut. Bryant had been Nemo's first handler.

Just before dawn on December 4, 1966, was a fatal time for sentry dogs and their handlers at Tan Son Nhut Air Base in Vietnam. Some Vietcong had gotten onto base property, killing one handler and three sentry dogs. The day passed with no further incidents. Then, shortly after midnight, sentry dog Nemo and his handler, Robert Thorneburg, discovered the Vietcong infiltrators hiding in a cemetery. Thorneburg released Nemo, who raced toward the enemies. Hearing shots and then Nemo yelping in pain, Thorneburg reacted, killing one Vietcong soldier before he was shot. Nemo managed to crawl to where Thorneburg fell and lay down on top of him. When reinforcements arrived, Nemo growled, protecting his handler. Finally, other handlers got him to leave so they could tend to the injured Thorneburg.

Both Thorneburg and Nemo recovered, but Nemo lost sight in one eye. Retired from duty, Nemo returned to the United States and traveled around the country, helping recruit dogs for the armed services. He died in 1972, partly as a result of the wounds he received that evening.

The Military Working Dog Finds Its Place

The Vietnam experience really helped the armed forces realize just how valuable the dogs' heightened senses can be. As Mike Dowling, a former Marine Corps handler, said, "You can only see what you can see. You can't see what you don't see. A dog can see it through his nose."

Handler/trainee Elizabeth Davis works with her dog, Maya, at the Lackland AFB training grounds.

Dogs excel at night-patrol work because of their superior night vision, sharp hearing, and keen sense of smell.

In 1972, Lackland Air Force Base in San Antonio, Texas, became the central place for training the different kinds of Military Working Dogs. Besides training for patrol duty, some dogs were taught to sniff out explosives or drugs. They could find hidden illegal weapons or drugs with ease, keeping military bases safe and drug free. Because of the great demand for MWDs, Lackland AFB began raising Belgian Malinois puppies. The Malinois has been bred as a working dog in Europe, and is a fine athlete that is quick to learn and eager to please, making it an ideal partner for the armed forces. The Dutch Shepherd, German Shepherd, and Labrador Retriever are also favored, and the British armed forces often use spaniels. But a dog's pedigree doesn't really matter. If any type of dog shows promise, it is welcome to serve.

Spc. Robert Dami and his spaniel MWD, Jay, play fetch.

★ From Puppy to MWD

From the time they are three days old, the puppies at Lackland receive plenty of attention to get them used to being handled. Attendants tickle the pups between their toes with cotton swabs and hold them in different ways. They stand the youngsters on damp, cool towels to expose them to a different surface. At eight weeks of age, each puppy gets an aptitude test. A promising puppy will eagerly come to people with its tail held high. It won't struggle when held on its back, and it will eagerly chase a ball and return it. It has a strong drive to hunt, doggedly sniffing out a hidden tray of puppy kibbles. It also has a strong attachment to a particular toy. This attachment becomes the key to becoming a successful MWD.

★ ★ ★ ★

This Malinois puppy
is ready to get moving!

Puppies born at Lackland are given names beginning with double letters to distinguish them from dogs from other sources. Ddonahue and Ddiaz, eight-week-old Malinois puppies, were named for handlers who lost their lives in war.

No matter that she already has a ball in her mouth, Rrespect wants another.
Her puppy raiser, Sarah Dietrich, encourages Rrespect in her love of toys
because it will help her become a good MWD.

The puppies that show promise go to live with foster families. The families must live within two hours of Lackland, because the puppies get monthly medical checkups there and join one another for activities like hikes.

The foster families expose the puppies to as many situations as possible—noisy sidelines at soccer games, smelly bus rides, restaurants with rich food odors. These dogs will need to be comfortable and confident in all sorts of environments when they go to work in order to do their job well.

When they are seven months old, the puppies are thoroughly tested again to see if they hold promise as MWDs. If they do, the families must say good-bye and return them to Lackland.

The puppies that don't show promise as MWDs are offered for adoption. First choice goes to the foster families that raised them. If the family doesn't take the dog, it's available to the general public.

Like many Lackland puppies, Nnordo is being raised by base personnel, in this case by Col. William H. Mott.

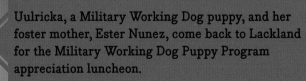

Uulricka, a Military Working Dog puppy, and her foster mother, Ester Nunez, come back to Lackland for the Military Working Dog Puppy Program appreciation luncheon.

★ Getting Ready to Learn

Now things get more serious for the puppies. They need to get used to living in a kennel. At first they miss their familiar homes and families. But soon things get very busy, as they start to focus on learning their jobs.

Each puppy gets a sturdy rubber toy called a KONG that it wants to carry everywhere. The puppy has to learn to give up its toy so that the trainer can hide it. There's a big room at Lackland full of desks and cupboards with lots of places where the toy could be hidden. The young dog sniffs out the toy and learns how to open doors and drawers to get it. Soon it is enjoying these games of hide and seek. It is learning a simple but vital lesson: searching for a particular odor will result in a reward. Once the dog understands how to hunt for its toy and find it, it's ready to learn to hunt for something more serious, such as dynamite or cocaine.

Rruuk's toy is an important tool for him to learn how to search.

An energetic litter of Malinois puppies greets kennel volunteer Senior Airman Tristan Hysaw at Lackland.

By searching for his toy, Rruuk learns how to open cabinets and drawers.

★ Basic Training

Because the need for dogs that can become good MWDs is so strong and the base-raised puppies are not enough, Lackland staff travel throughout the US and Europe to find young dogs with the right traits for military careers to join the Lackland puppies for training.

All MWDs must first learn basic obedience commands, like sit, stay, come, and lie down, following both voice and hand signals. They all learn to tolerate loud sounds. Once they master these essentials, some are trained to recognize the smells of explosives and weapons, while others specialize in illegal drug detection.

Others will become patrol dogs, learning to search on leash for weapons and explosives. They will work on military bases, in war zones, and at locations where important government officials will be visiting.

Cpl. Angelo Melendez gives the command to roll over to his MWD, Rocky. Handlers spend many hours a day training their dogs, even while on other duty.

Their Bite *Is* Worse Than Their Bark

British attack dog Balu shows off the padded sleeve he has successfully torn away from a simulated attacker.

The typical MWD is trained to attack a fleeing suspect and hold him. The dog learns to run after a person walking away, bite a thick protective arm sleeve, and hang on until commanded by its handler to let go.

These MWDs are selected partly on the basis of their desire to bite and chew toys and play tug of war. When they perform correctly in the training, they are rewarded by being given the sleeve to chew on and play with. What drives them to bite isn't viciousness or the desire to hurt someone—it's praise from their handlers and the pleasure they feel while chewing on and playing with the sleeve.

Complete obedience is vital in bite training. The dog must let go immediately when commanded "out," and must sit or lie down quickly upon command.

As training continues, the dogs learn to grab suspects by the leg if necessary to stop them, and to guard suspects and hold them in place until their handlers catch up.

This MWD-in-training jumps high to grab the bite sleeve.

Petty Officer Jeremiah Boone insists that the dog sit after releasing the bite sleeve during training.

27

Training the Handlers

The most intensively trained MWDs are called SSDs, short for Specialized Search Dogs. They search off leash for explosives. These dogs work with handlers who also receive detailed training, and the team of dog and handler stay together throughout their years of service.

The SSD handler recruits are trained separately from their dogs. At first the recruits are given a leash, a collar, and a metal can that represents their dog. They learn how to put on the collar and how to handle the leash. They also have to learn how to reward their dogs with enthusiastic praise. Just saying "Good girl" in a quiet voice isn't enough. Handlers must learn to express great enthusiasm at each of their dog's accomplishments by practicing with their can "dogs." Once the handlers learn to praise their cans energetically, they can easily praise their dogs that way!

Sgt. John Oyervides praises his MWD, Hyk, for his good work.

Next, the handler trainees learn to work with real dogs that have already trained but were unsuitable for the challenging MWD work, due to injury or some other reason.

After thirty days of training, each new SSD handler takes one of the training dogs through an obedience course with various barriers. They also must get the dog to search a car the right way. They need to show that they can manage the dog correctly, even if it is reluctant to cooperate. During this test, only the handlers are being judged, not the dogs.

USAF Senior Airman Brandon Hinton orders his patrol dog, War, to go through the tunnel on the K9 obstacle course.

MWD handler Staff Sgt. Scott Bronnbauer guides his Belgian Malinois partner, Eddie, over an obstacle at the K9 training facility on Scott Air Force Base, Illinois.

Sgt. Elizabeth Wienke is tested at Lackland for her ability to get Zok to search a car correctly.

This MWD-in-training is being tested on its ability to fetch in a simulated war situation.

★ ★ ★ ★ ★

Once they have shown they can work effectively with dogs, the SSD handlers-in-training start to work with the dogs that will end up as SSDs. Each trainee gets two dogs to work with at Lackland for a month. There, both the handlers and the dogs learn about the different environments and explosives they might encounter. They stumble together through "environmental rooms" strewn with garbage, old tires, boxes, ladders—all sorts of litter. They explore a pretend Afghan home and a model of an explosives-making lab. The dogs are taught to recognize nine or more dangerous chemicals used to make bombs.

An SSD-in-training gets used to working on uneven surfaces in an environmental room at Lackland AFB.

SSD handlers learn what a bomb-making lab might look like, and the dogs learn what they might smell like, in this mock-up at Lackland AFB.

After a month, the handlers must choose. Which of their dogs works best for them? Which will they take along to protect their comrades from harm? After the handler chooses, the second dog returns to the pool of available dogs. Then the handlers and their chosen canine partners continue training together.

Finally, the SSD teams travel to the Arizona desert for two weeks, where they practice in the hot, dry weather in various environments, such as a mock hostile rural village.

Features:

Intruder Antenna
• fully integrated in K9 Storm Vest
• rugged
• folding

Intruder Special Ops. Handle, Kevlar Load Bearing V-Rings, Patented Built-In Harness System
• fast-roping, parachuting, rappelling, lifting & lowering
• track, search, apprehend

Intruder Camera
• Lexan Strike Shield lens protection
• built-in night vision
• designed for tunnel, cave, fortified building searches, & SWAT Operations

Intruder Arm
• 180 degrees of movement
• solid stainless steel pivot point
• streamlined design, folds down flat when not in use
• gross motor skills activation, can be opened with one hand

Intruder Battery Pak & Magazine
• 4 channel user selectable from transmitter & receiver
• magazine can be changed in seconds in zero light conditions

Intruder Outer Carrier
• ideal drainage for amphibious assault ops.

Intruder On-Off Switch
• encapsulated
• gross motor skills activated
• fully integrated

The K9 Storm Intruder™ vest has many useful features.

32

MWDs wear "doggles" to protect their eyes when they jump from aircraft.

MWDs learn to carry out many different kinds of missions, depending on what's needed. Some even learn to jump fearlessly from an aircraft and float to earth on a parachute in case they are needed in a remote location. Depending on their assignment, the dogs may need special equipment. They might wear cooling vests in the desert and goggles, called "doggles," to protect their eyes from the sand. A dog may wear heavy assault armor for protection in battle. A vest can even carry GPS equipment, gear that can use radio uplinks to record data, or a light to help the camera see what's happening inside a dark building.

Some reports say that dogs used by the highly trained, elite Special Forces units, like the one that took part in the Osama bin Laden raid, wear such vests. Special Forces teams do their own MWD training in secret. Outsiders do not know the specific facts about what the dogs are trained to do, but they probably learn at least the same basic commands and jobs that other MWDs carry out, wear the same gear—and more.

Cindy wears booties to protect her feet from cold and ice.

★ The Right Dog for the Job

All the US military forces use MWDs in various ways. The dogs and handlers for SSD work are all trained at Lackland AFB. Most other MWDs also train at Lackland, but the handlers are trained on their home bases. After training, the dogs are sent from Lackland to the various bases, where they are matched up with their handlers. Mine Detection Dogs (MDDs), often Labrador Retrievers, are trained at Fort Leonard Wood in Missouri. The Marines in Afghanistan also work with Labrador Retrievers trained by private contractors. This hunting breed is famous for its great sense of smell, intelligence, and obedience, which enable the dogs to work off leash with their handlers.

Now and then, a special kind of dog is needed for a special job. Submarines have cramped spaces and narrow vertical ladders connecting decks. A big dog like a shepherd would never do for searching such a ship. Instead, terriers like Lars get the job. Lars is small enough to be easily carried up and down a sub's ladders.

Lars (right), posing with a fellow US Navy MWD, is the perfect size for his submarine assignment.

Sometimes, the job of MWD is not the right fit for a dog. MWDs must be highly motivated to work for their rewards—their toys and/or praise from their handlers—and must have a strong hunting instinct. They also need to be physically strong and hardy. Sometimes they must work for long hours at a stretch without losing interest or getting too tired. It's a very demanding job, both for the handler and the dog. Some dogs just aren't quite up to the demands of military service, and are offered first to law enforcement agencies. If there are no takers, the dog is made available for adoption, either by its handler or a private family. An MWD that is ready to retire, either because of health issues or age, is also available for adoption by MWD handlers or the general public.

Dogs like this one standing on a bluff overlooking an Afghan village are used by private contractors to find dangerous land mines.

35

★ In the War Zone

Once MWD teams deploy, their lives change dramatically. Now the danger is real, not pretend. The lives of the men and women in a patrol all depend on the dog to keep them safe. The gunfire and bombs are deadly.

The bond that formed as the team trained together becomes stronger and stronger in the field. Out in the countryside there are no kennels, and the handler has full responsibility for taking care of his dog day and night. Dog and handler alike know that one will do everything possible to protect the other.

A marine in Afghanistan shares a special celebration steak dinner with his MWD as his buddy looks on.

US Army Staff Sgt. Frederick Ferrigno bathes his dog, Hugo, at a camp overseas in 2010.

This MWD has a tough job—finding missing soldiers—but affection from a fellow soldier helps to comfort both of them.

For all soldiers in a war environment, the steady love and loyalty of a dog, wagging its tail happily at the thought of a treat or a pat on the head even after long hours of scary and often noisy work, helps keep up the spirits of the troops.

Marine Corps LCpl. Colton Rusk (see facing page) and his MWD, Eli, were inseparable partners day and night.

AFGHANISTAN WAR HERO HOUND: ELI

Tragedy can sometimes cause a dog to retire. Marine Corps LCpl. Colton Rusk and his MWD, Eli, were at work in a dangerous part of Afghanistan in December 2010 when Colton was shot and fell to the ground. Eli crawled to his partner and lay over his body to protect him, but Colton died.

Whenever Colton used to phone home, he'd always update everyone on Eli's antics. Even though Eli was only four years old and in good health, the Marine Corps decided to retire him from service so that Colton's family could adopt him. At the adoption ceremony at Lackland AFB in early February 2011, Eli snuggled up with the family as if he recognized their relationship to Colton. Now Eli lives in a small Texas town with the Rusks and three canine buddies, providing a loving bridge between Colton and his grieving family.

Eli licks the face of his new "brother," Brady, the twelve-year-old brother of fallen marine Colton Rusk.

A Nose for Danger

A marine and his Dutch Shepherd MWD head out to work in Afghanistan.

The most important job of MWDs in both the second Iraq war and the war in Afghanistan has been detecting roadside bombs, also called IEDs, short for "improvised explosive devices." These deadly weapons are hidden or buried along and beneath the surface of roads and pathways and explode when weight from a person or vehicle is put on them. Dogs are able to detect IEDs with amazing accuracy, and can find three of them in less than an hour. More than 60 percent of the deaths of coalition forces in both Iraq and Afghanistan have been caused by these weapons. Estimates are that each SSD saves 150 lives during its service. Sergeant Richard Miller explains that searching for explosives is nerve-wracking. But when the dog finds an IED, it's exciting to know that all the hard work and training paid off—this dog can keep soldiers safe.

MWDs also search around and inside buildings to find weapons stashes, explosive devices, or people in hiding. "What if Osama [bin Laden] had been hiding in a hole in the ground?" asks former MWD handler Mike Dowling. "A dog could alert them to where he's hiding because of the incredible scent capabilities." Another advantage of using dogs to search is speed—a dog can search a car eight times faster than a person can.

British and Australian soldiers also use what they call Arms and Explosive Search (AES) dogs in the field. Since most British units include dogs, all soldiers bound for Afghanistan have been trained with military dogs.

Cpl. Michael Zarate and his drug-detection dog, Roy, search a building for drugs and anyone evading arrest at the compound of a known Taliban commander and drug trafficker.

AFGHANISTAN WAR HERO HOUND: SABI

Sabi, an Australian Explosive Detection Dog, worked in Afghanistan until she went missing during a fire fight. Her human comrades searched and searched to no avail and finally declared her missing in battle. Fourteen months later, an American soldier found her wandering around in a remote area and returned her to her unit, where she was hailed as a dog hero. After returning to Australia, Sabi was awarded the RSPCA's Purple Cross, Australia's most prestigious award for animal bravery.

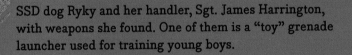

SSD dog Ryky and her handler, Sgt. James Harrington, with weapons she found. One of them is a "toy" grenade launcher used for training young boys.

Keeping Dogs Healthy

Like their human companions, MWDs can be injured in training or in battle. Every effort is made to keep the dogs healthy and able to work. But if a dog is injured or ill, it is sent to the Holland Military Working Dog Hospital at Lackland to recover. Injuries are treated with surgery as needed, and the hospital has state-of-the-art rehabilitation equipment, such as a water tank with a treadmill. An injured dog can start getting back into shape gently in this tank, then graduate to a regular treadmill when its injured limb can take its full weight. Muscles weakened by disuse from surgery can be stimulated electrically to help strengthen them.

This injured MWD is being exercised on a treadmill in a water-filled tank. The water helps take weight off the injured leg while its muscles are strengthened.

Afghanistan Hero Hound Gina with Master Sgt. Eric Haynes, who helped her recover from PTSD.

AFGHANISTAN WAR HERO HOUND: GINA

Sometimes military canines, like human fighters, can develop fear-based psychological symptoms. This condition is called post-traumatic stress disorder (PTSD). Both people and dogs with PTSD may be jumpy at loud sounds, have terrifying nightmares, be afraid of crowded places or new environments, or show other symptoms.

After five months in Iraq, where an IED exploded right behind her vehicle, Gina developed PTSD. Gina was terrified by just about everything and could no longer be relied upon to find explosives.

She returned to Peterson Air Force Base in Colorado, where Master Sergeant Eric Haynes began helping Gina heal. He started gradually, walking with her to stores on the base. At first Gina cowered at the sight of an approaching person. Sergeant Haynes had treats passed out to people in the stores, who then gave them to Gina so she would begin to trust people again. Every day the pair would walk around the base, and Gina began to get used to the normal sounds of people and cars again. Then, bit by bit, she became accustomed to the sound of gunfire on the training grounds.

Once again, Gina has become a playful dog who enjoys her work. She now has a new handler, Staff Sergeant Melinda Miller. The pair works on base, patrolling and doing detection work. Eventually, Gina may be able to return to the front, where she can once again help save human lives.

★ Looking to the Future

MWDs are now vital partners in the military during peacetime as well as wartime. Their ability to detect any odor makes them the only real protection against explosive devices, since these are now commonly made with no metal parts. For example, although American forces have left Iraq, Military Working Dogs have not. In 2010, the United States military donated 270 dogs for Iraqi security, and Iraqi officials say they will need around six hundred of these dogs into the future. Around the world, police and military forces are acquiring explosive-detecting dogs to help them cope with terrorist threats and rebel activities. The Department of Homeland Security is starting to use bomb-sniffing dogs and plans on training about six hundred of them.

Since dogs can also learn a variety of other defense-related tasks, such as tracking people, detecting dead bodies, and serving as sentries, they carry out multiple roles in protective services, such as search and rescue after a disaster.

By late 2011, United States forces had 2,700 dogs on active duty. The training facility at Lackland Air Force Base is expecting to train around five hundred dogs a year, with no end in sight. The goal of the puppy-raising program there is eventually to provide about 30 percent of US MWDs.

MWD Randy works with his handler, US Army Spc. Dennis Bechtel, in a hunt for weapon caches near an Iraqi village.

RETIRED IRAQ HERO HOUND: BINO

Bino, whose formal name was MWD Bino C152, served as a Narcotics Detection/Patrol K9 dog at Fort Gordon in Georgia for almost eleven years. He also spent fourteen months in Iraq protecting the troops as well as having special missions in Texas and Arizona detecting drugs for the Border Patrol.

After retirement, Bino found a new job as a trainer, helping veterans who suffer from PTSD and their service dogs learn how to work together in the busy world. Bino and his adoptive owner, Debbie Kandoll, guided veterans and their new service dogs through noisy malls, cramped elevators, and other real-world situations so that the dogs could calmly help their veterans deal with what could otherwise be anxious situations. In 2011, Bino was one of eight finalists for the Hero Dog Award, given by the American Humane Association, for service beyond the call of duty. Bino, who passed away in early 2012, showed that dogs can keep on giving willingly to others for their entire lives.

Many of the skills learned by MWDs can also be used to help rescue civilians in natural disasters, like finding people buried under collapsed buildings after earthquakes.

★ Further Resources

Websites

http://www.defense.gov/home/features/2006/working-dogs/
Official MWD site of the US Department of Defense

http://www.lackland.af.mil/units/341stmwd/index.asp
Main page for the various MWD aspects of Lackland AFB

http://community-2.webtv.net/Hahn-50thAP-K9/K9History/
A detailed history of dogs and war from early history up until the end of the twentieth century, with detailed information about many different eras

Books for Young Readers

Dennis, Major Brian, Kirby Larson, and Mary Nethery. *Nubs: The True Story of a Mutt, a Marine & a Miracle.*
    New York: Little, Brown Books for Young Readers, 2009.
About a street dog in Iraq who won the heart of a Marine.

Jackson, Donna M. *Hero Dogs: Courageous Canines in Action.* New York: Scholastic Book Services, 2004.
An overview of heroic dogs both in the military and civilian sectors.

Kadohata, Cynthia. *Cracker! The Best Dog in Vietnam.* New York: Atheneum Books for Young Readers, 2008.
A fictional account of a war dog in the Vietnam War.

Ruffin, Frances E. *Military Dogs (Dog Heroes).* New York: Bearport Publishing, 2006.
An introduction to dogs in the military.

★ Glossary

AES dog: British Arms and Explosive Search dog; often a spaniel, chosen for its sensitive sense of smell.

EDD: Term for an Australian Explosive Detection Dog.

IED: Improvised Explosive Device, or roadside bomb.

MDD: Mine Detection Dog, trained to find land mines and buried unexploded ordnance. Trained at Fort Leonard Wood, Missouri; handled by combat engineers.

Messenger dog: WWI dog who trusted two handlers, one on the front and one at headquarters. It carried vital messages and small supplies back and forth through enemy lines.

MWD: Military Working Dog, a general term that includes dogs trained for different duties.

Patrol Dog: Dog that works at a military base, especially at night.

Scout dog: Silent dog that led combat patrols on leash and warned of danger.

Sentry dog: A dog trained to warn of danger by barking or growling.

SSD: Specialized Search Dog, trained to find firearms, ammunition, and explosives during searches along roads, in buildings and vehicles, and in open areas. Always works under direct control of handler.

★ Index

Note: *Italic* page numbers indicate photographs.

Photo Credits

All photographs, except for those credited below, are courtesy of the various branches of the Department of Defense.
Lance Cheung/Legion Photo: 20; courtesy of LCDR John E. Gay, US Navy: 34; Sgt. James Harrington: 41 (bottom); K9 Storm: 4, 6, 32; Jerry Lara/*The San Antonio Express-News*/ZUMA: 39 (bottom); Library of Congress: 8 (top left and bottom), 9; Matthew Mahon Photo, LLC/Redux Pictures: 43; courtesy of Carl Montgomery: 35; National Archives: 10, 11 (bottom [both]), 12, 13, 14 (top), 15; Michael Partenio, courtesy of Debbie Kandoll: 45 (top); Dorothy Hinshaw Patent: 14 (bottom), 16 (right), 18, 27 (bottom), 29 (bottom), 31 (both), 48; courtesy of the Rusk family: 38 (bottom), 39 (top); Wikimedia Commons: 8 (top right), 11 (top)

To Kathy Cross for the idea, and to Emily Easton, for making it happen

Copyright © 2012 by Dorothy Hinshaw Patent

First published in the United States of America in September 2012 by Walker Publishing Company, Inc., a division of Bloomsbury Publishing, Inc.
www.bloomsburykids.com

For information about permission to reproduce selections from this book, write to Permissions, Walker BFYR, 175 Fifth Avenue, New York, New York 10010

Library of Congress Cataloging-in-Publication Data available upon request
ISBN 978-0-8027-2845-6 (hardcover)
ISBN 978-0-8027-2846-3 (reinforced)

Typeset in Bodoni Egyption
Book design by Regina Roff

Printed in China by by Hung Hing Printing (China) Co., Ltd., Shenzhen, Guangdong
(hardcover) 10 9 8 7 6 5 4 3 2 1
(reinforced) 10 9 8 7 6 5 4 3 2 1

All papers used by Bloomsbury Publishing, Inc., are natural, recyclable products made from wood grown in well-managed forests. The manufacturing processes conform to the environmental regulations of the country of origin.

Sources

I received official Book Support from the US Air Force, which allowed me to visit Lackland Air Force Base for firsthand research, and also from the Army, Marines, and Navy, so that I could conduct phone interviews with members of the various armed forces. Please see the acknowledgments for specifics about those who so willingly shared their time and knowledge with me.

I used many websites for information and photos, including those in Further Resources. In addition, these sites were especially helpful resources for research, but not always appropriate for viewing by younger readers:

http://doglawreporter.blogspot.com
www.marines.mil/news/Pages/photos.aspx
www.militaryworkingdogs.com/history.shtml
www.qmfound.com/K-9.htm
http://ricks.foreignpolicy.com/category/one_time_tags/rebeccas_
    war_dog_of_the_week
www.uswardogs.org
www.visualintel.net/SpecialTopics/Military-Working-Dog

Acknowledgments

Special thanks to Gerry Proctor, 37th Training Wing public affairs, Lackland Air Force Base, who arranged my tour and interviews and provided much additional help by e-mail; and Michael Lemish, former historian for the Vietnam War Dog Handlers Association, by e-mail and through his book *War Dogs: A History of Loyalty and Heroism* (Washington DC: Potomac Books, 1999).

I also want to thank the many helpful people at Lackland AFB who provided valuable information for the book: Petty Officer Jeremiah Boone, Dr. Walter F. Burghardt, Jimmy Dalton, Sgt. Elizabeth Davis, John Engstrom, CMSgt Michael Fluck, SPC Tyler B. Gosla, Dr. Stewart Hilliard, Col. Kelly Mann, SSG Richard H. Miller, Orlando Nuñez, Tech. Sgt. David Reavis, MSgt Richard Reidel, and Major Wm. Roberts.

The following people also contributed helpful information: Jim Slater (K9 Storm Inc.), Debbie Kandoll, Kathy Rusk, LCDR John E. Gay (US Navy), Master Chief Scott Thompson (US Navy), Capt. Gregory A. Wolf (USMC), Capt. Brian Block (USMC), GySgt Greg Massey (USMC), Sgt. James Harrington (US Army, retired), and Bob Himrod.